Dig It Out

Katie Spina

DEDICATION

For all my Awesome Authors Kids
who inspire me to write from the heart.

For my son, Darwin
who gives me reasons to keep feeling big feelings.

And lastly, for my dad
who grew to accept those "stupid stories" were my destiny.

ACKNOWLEDGMENTS

There are so many people that make a project happen. Thank you to my husband for always supporting my writing dream. Thank you to my wonderful support system (you amazing women know who you are). I couldn't do half of what I do without your love and support.

Gigi was a groundhog who loved to dig. Being little in a world made for grown-ups was confusing at times, but digging always made sense.

Gigi's favorite thing in the world was her blue sweater with shiny silver buttons. She put it on like a warm coat of armor. Nothing could harm Brave Knight Gigi wearing her armor. It made her brave enough to walk past the neighbor's mean dog. It made her kind enough to help the gray lady pick up her dropped books. It made her powerful enough to climb the highest fences.

One day, Brave Knight Gigi lost her armor. She searched everywhere for her favorite sweater: in the laundry hamper; at the back of her closet; under the couch cushions. Her armor was gone. She flopped onto the grass in her backyard. Without her armor, the back fence was too high to climb. Gigi missed her sweater so much her heart hurt.

To get away from the sadness, Gigi started to dig. It felt good to dig. Gigi dug as day gave way to night and the stars crept out one by one. Gigi didn't want to stop. If she was digging, she didn't feel how sad she was. All her memories stayed behind her up in the grass.

Gigi dug for hours. Her muscles worked hard. Her mind was clear. She was ready to dig forever, but the Earth isn't dirt all the way down. Gigi found bedrock. She hit her furry fist against the solid layer of rock. There was nowhere else to dig.

Gigi missed her sweater. The soil around her was cold and wet.
With her sweater, she would be warm. Instead, she was trapped
in a hole, unable to dig away from the sadness.

Gigi sat in the quiet. Alone in the dark, the sadness found her. Gigi looked up through the deep pit she had made. Out in the sky, the stars twinkled in their nighttime beds. The stars were further away than usual. Gigi started to cry. The stars hadn't moved. They were in the same places they always were. Gigi was further away.

Gigi thought about the adventures she'd never have. How would she walk to the library without her magic shield to protect from wild animals? How would she be brave enough to help a stranger as Plain Gigi?

Gigi looked up again. The night sky was lovely. The stars winked at her. They used to wink like that on her chilly night walks. Wearing her favorite sweater, Brave Knight Gigi had the strength to walk around the whole wide world.

Grass around the top of the pit moved in the wind. The rock under Gigi was hard. The sadness made her whole body hurt. Gigi got angry. She kicked the side of the pit. She couldn't dig down, but that didn't mean she couldn't keep digging.

Gigi pushed her claws into the soil and pulled the fresh earth to her. She started a tunnel in the side of her hole. Gigi climbed inside and kept moving away from her feelings.

She thrust her claws out and pulled soil to her, pushing it out behind her. Her muscles loved to move. She made the tunnel just big enough that she could slide her large groundhog body through it. The soil was damp and cold against her belly. Gigi smelled the freshly-turned dirt. Digging was much easier than feeling.

The tunnel couldn't go on forever. Bedrock stopped the hole. Daylight stopped the tunnel. Cracks of sunshine poked through the soil above Gigi's head. Her digging was ending again. She would have to face her feelings again.

Gigi breathed in the safe smell of the soil around her. She closed her eyes against the ribbons of brightness. In the light, she thought about the good memories with her sweater.

She remembered climbing the impossible tree to get her cousin's kite. Her sweater had been tied around her neck like a cape. That day, Brave Knight Gigi was a superhero.

Then she remembered the sleepover at Grandma's last summer. Gigi's sweater was in the washer because it had gotten muddy. The bedroom was dark. Gigi was scared of the dark. She wanted to call out for Grandma, but that wasn't how a Brave Knight acted. A Brave Knight faced their fears.

Gigi had always felt powerful wearing her sweater, but the power wasn't in the sweater. The power was in Gigi. It was always inside Gigi. With her happy memories to wrap around her, and her self-love to heal her broken heart, Gigi was ready to face the daylight again.

Gigi thrust a fist into the nearest crack of brightness above her head. One big deep breath later, she had broken through the surface.

Brave Knight Gigi was ready to face the world, armor or no.

18

ABOUT THE AUTHOR

Photo © Cute but Psycho Photography

Ms. Katie is a reader first and a writer second. Books have always been her favorite vacation. Like Gigi, the world was confusing when Ms. Katie was little, but books always made sense. Her greatest hope is that kids will see themselves in the characters she creates.

Made in the USA
Lexington, KY
06 May 2018